For Annie — on her
birthday, July 21, 1999
with our love —
Grandpa & Grandmom

For Annie — on her
birthday, July 21, 1999
with our love —
Grandpa & Grandmom

Captain's Castaway

By Angeli Perrow
Pictures by Emily Harris

Down East Books / Camden, Maine

Down East Books
P.O Box 679, Camden, ME 04843

BOOK ORDERS: 800-766-1670

LIBRARY OF CONGRESS CATALOGING-IN-PUBLICATION DATA

Perrow, Angeli, 1954—
    Captain's castaway / story by Angeli Perrow ; illustrations by Emily Harris.
        p.   cm.
    Summary : When a storm at sea causes a shipwreck, the captain's injured dog
finds its way to shore where the young daughter of the lighthouse keeper rescues and
befriends it.
    ISBN 0-89272-419-6
    1. Dogs—Juvenile fiction. [1. Dogs—Fiction. 2. Shipwrecks—Fiction.
3. Lighthouses—Fiction.] I. Harris, Emily, 1951—
ill. II. Title.
PZ10.3.P31345Cap 1998
[E]—dc21
                                                                98-34914
                                                                   CIP
                                                                    AC

For Ariel, my lighthouse girl

The captain's dog braced his legs on the rolling deck of the ship. Sea spray misted his curly yellow fur with an all-over halo.

He was a good dog,
a caring dog,
a daring dog,
a sea dog.

A seagull wheeled and reeled in the
freshening breeze. It landed on the
ship's rail. The captain's dog
bounded across the deck
and barked a warning
at the bird. No
stranger—be it bird
or beast—would board his ship.

He sniffed the air. A storm was coming for sure. He barked to warn the crew. The sailors hurried, the sailors scurried to take in the sails.

Abigail

He was a good dog,
a frolicking dog,
a rollicking dog,
a sea dog.

The sky grew dark as night. The waves crashed against the sides of the shuddering ship. The captain's dog sensed danger ahead. For the third time he barked.

Just then the lookout cried from the crow's nest above, "A light, dead ahead!"

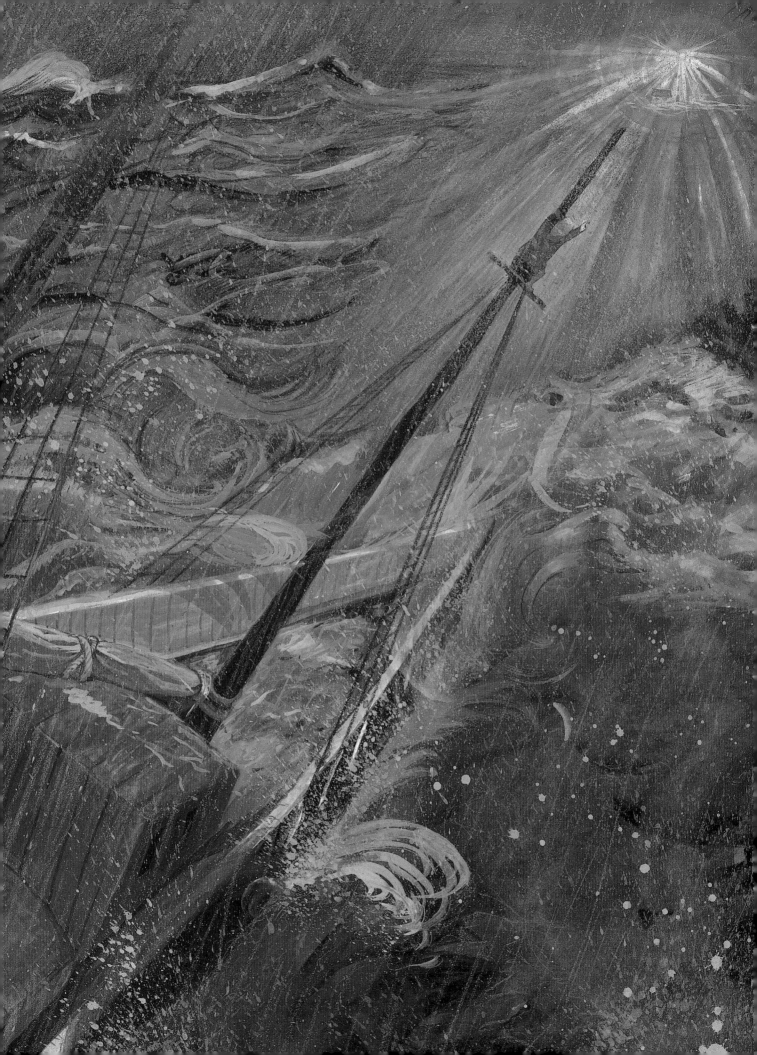

The helmsman pulled the ship's wheel
hard to starboard, but it was too late.
Wooden planks crunched on hidden rocks.
"Man the lifeboats!" shouted the captain.
The men scrambled into the boats and
lowered themselves into the angry sea.

The captain's dog jumped into the wild waves
and paddled to a lifeboat. He put his paws
on the side and tried to wiggle in.

The lifeboat began to tip. "He's going to sink us!" yelled a sailor, and he knocked the dog back into the sea with an oar.

The boat surged past the dog. The oar had injured him, but he bravely swam for his life.

He was a good dog,
a brave dog,
a trying-to-save-himself dog,
a sea dog.

The light the lookout had glimpsed was Great Duck Island Lighthouse. The sailors rowed until their lifeboats scraped the shore. They crawled out and sprawled on the land.

They scrambled through the wind and rain to
the lighthouse. The keeper and his wife greeted
the shipwrecked sailors with warm blankets and
hot coffee.

The next day, the keeper ferried the crew to the mainland in his own boat. The captain's dog was given up as lost at sea.

The keeper and his wife had a daughter. Often she escaped from her many brothers and sisters to do things by herself.

Sarah was a lonely girl,
a roving girl,
a looking-for-a-friend girl,
a lighthouse girl.

Her favorite time to explore the beach was after a storm. She never knew what she might find! Her brown eyes sparkled as she thought about the time she found a perfect moon shell.

She had placed the pearly spiral to her ear and heard the distant *shush-shush* of the sea inside the shell. It was her favorite treasure.

Sarah flicked her long braids over her shoulder
as she searched the flotsam and jetsam of the
shore the day after the shipwreck. She was poking
at a tangle of rope with a stick when she heard a
sound like a baby crying. It seemed to be coming
from the rocks.

Curious, she peered between two barnacle-encrusted rocks. At first, she saw only a mass of matted yellow fur.

Then the creature lifted its head and looked at her with soft, brown eyes.

"A dog," Sarah breathed. "And he's hurt!"

With her long skirts flying, Sarah ran for
help. Returning to the shore, she and her father
carefully placed the dog on a blanket and
carried him to the house.

Sarah used the blanket to form a cozy nest by the woodstove. She bathed the dog and dried him and fed him and soothed him. She bandaged his injured paw.

Sarah was a nursing girl,
a needed girl,
a never-let-you-down girl,
a lighthouse girl.

"Because you are a gift from the sea," Sarah announced, "I name you Seaboy."

As the girl went about her chores, the dog followed her with his eyes. In a few days he was limping after her. Before long he was constantly at her side. Together they worked, they played— companions glad and true.

Two years later, the sea captain returned to Great Duck Island to thank the keeper for his help. As the two men stood talking, Sarah and Seaboy came into sight.

"That's my dog!" exclaimed the captain. "I thought he had drowned!"

"He nearly did," said the keeper. "Sarah found him and saved his life."

Sarah knelt beside Seaboy and buried her face in his yellow fur. She didn't want the men to see her tears. It was only natural that the captain would want his dog back.

"Here, boy!" called the captain.

Seaboy barked happily and raced to the man.
He climbed into the dory, and the captain
shoved off from shore.
   Sarah's heart was breaking. Her best friend
was leaving.
   "Seaboy!" she cried.

Seaboy's ears perked up. He bounded from the small boat and swam back to Sarah. He sat at her feet and gazed at her with trusting eyes.

"Here, boy!" called the captain again.

Seaboy wagged his tail but he stayed beside Sarah.

The captain chuckled. "Well, I can see he has found a good home and a good friend."

He was a good boy,
a grateful boy,
a faithful boy,
a Seaboy.

Sarah was a fun girl,
a faithful girl,
a friend-forever girl,
a lighthouse girl.

There were many shipwrecks along the rugged
Maine coast in the 1800s. According to lighthouse
historians, the story of Seaboy is a true tale. There
really was a dog who was knocked into the water by
the oar of a panicky sailor. Although injured, he
managed to swim to shore.

The real name of the girl is not known, but she
was the daughter of a lighthouse keeper on Great
Duck Island. She did name the dog Seaboy after
finding him on the shore and nursing him back to
health.

The ship's captain did eventually return to the
island and recognize Seaboy, but he allowed the girl
to keep the dog.